tiny titans

Adventures in Awesomeness

tiny

Adve

Awes

ntures in omeness

Art Baltazar & Franco
Writers

Art Baltazar
Artist & Letterer

Cover by Art Baltazar
TINY TITANS: ADVENTURES IN AWESOMENESS

DC Comics, 2900 W. Alameda Avenue, Burbank, CA 91505
Printed by LSC Communications, Salem, VA, USA. 2/3/17. Seventh Printing.
ISBN: 978-1-4012-2328-1

Library of Congress Cataloging-in-Publication Data

Baltazar, Art.
Adventures in awesomeness / Art Baltazar ; Franco.
pages cm. -- (Tiny Titans ; volume 2)
ISBN 9781401223281 (pbk.)
1. Graphic novels. I. Aureliani, Franco, illustrator. II. Title.
PZ7.7.B33 Tg 2009
741.5'973--dc23
2009280623

PEFC Certified
Printed on paper from sustainably managed forests, controlled sources
PEFC
PEFC/29-31-337
www.pefc.org

ROBIN

(Dick Grayson)- The brave and serious leader of the Tiny Titans. Although he is the original Robin, he is very moody and has to share his room with his brothers, the other Robins. Also, he has secret crushes for Starfire and Barbara Gordon.

The youngest of the three Robins. Too young to go to school, Jason is always in a happy mood and has a care-free style. He's all about smiling and having fun.

TIM DRAKE

The cool Robin. Tim wants to stand out from his brothers by wearing his own unique Robin costume. He's very laid back and easy going indeed.

KID FLASH

The super speedster and fastest kid in the school. Quick witted and eats lots for lunch because of his high metabolism. Too much candy will cause major sugar rush.

AQUALAD

The little boy from the ocean. Has a pet fish named Fluffy. Aqualad can communicate with all forms of sea life, even the pet hamster in their classroom.

SPEEDY

Quiet and cool, he is the boy with the trick arrows. He's good at anything that requires aiming. Also, he's Kid Flash's best friend.

WONDER GIRL

(Donna) Raised by amazons. She's strong and cute. Never lie to her, she has a magical jump rope which makes people tell the truth. Very skeptic.

RAVEN

The quiet and mysterious little girl. She really likes to experiment with dark magic, which usually turn into bad practical jokes. Mr. Trigon, the substitute teacher is her father.

CYBORG

Half boy, half robot. Cyborg is always tinkering with mechanical gadgets, often turning them into something else. His battle cry "BOO-YA!" has earned him the nickname, "Big Boo-Ya".

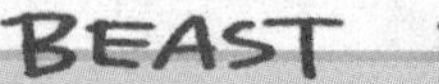

BEAST BOY

The green little boy who can change into any animal he desires. He's a prankster and loves comics. Has a crush on Terra.

STARFIRE

She's an alien princess. Very naïve and free spirited and finds the good in others. Has a crush on Robin and thinks he's cute, but so do all the other girls.

KID DEVIL

One of the younger Tiny Titans, still too young for school. Cannot talk but can breathe fire, usually while coughing or sneezing or hiccupping.

ROSE & JERICHO

Principal Slade's kids. Rose is the older and tougher "Tom-Boy" of the two. Jericho can't speak, but can take over your mind if you look into his eyes.

MISS MARTIAN

A shape shifting little girl alien from Mars who is still too young to go to school. She is often mistaken for Beast Boy's little sister.

TERRA

The sometimes hated little girl who likes to throw rocks. Principal Slade's teacher's pet. She thinks Beast Boy is a weirdo.

CASSIE

Wonder Girl's rich cousin from the big city. Cassie's really into fashion and is hip to all the latest trends in POP culture.

BUMBLE BEE

The tiniest of the Tiny Titans.
BB buzzes and packs a mighty stinger.

Because You Demanded it!

Titans in Space

tiny titans

PRINCIPAL SLADE'S OFFICE

SO, WHAT DID YOU DO?

CASSIE

KID DEVIL

PLASMUS

SHIMMER

GIZMO

PSIMON

AQUALAD

CYBORG

STARFIRE

RAVEN

KID FLASH

MISS MARTIAN

MAMMOTH

TERRA

BEAST BOY

ROBIN

WONDER GIRL

BUMBLEBEE

JERICHO

ROSE

SPEEDY

tiny titans
"YA THINK?"
IT'S YOUR MOVE.
I'M THINKING.

IT'S STILL YOUR MOVE.
I'M THINKING.

WALK WALK WALK WALK

IT'S YOUR MOVE.
I'M THINKING.

WOULD ONE OF YOU BRAINIACS JUST MAKE A MOVE ALREADY?!

HA HEE HOH!
SHE CALLS YOU BRAINIAC TOO!

No! No! No! MY NAME'S NOT, BRAINIAC!
THAT'S A TOTALLY DIFFERENT GUY!

IT'S YOUR MOVE, BRAINIAC.
I'M THINKING.

tiny titans
AW YEAH TITANS!

TEXT -DING-

HHMMM...

WHAT'S UP, STAR?
I JUST GOT A TEXT MESSAGE FROM MY DAD. I HAVE TO GO AND CLEAN MY ROOM.

ALLLL... THE WAY HOME?

YEP, ALL THE WAY TO PLANET TAMARAN.

SEE YA IN FIVE DAYS!

WANNA GO?

MINUTES LATER...

titans

HOLD ON TIGHT! TAKEOFF MIGHT BE A LITTLE BUMPY.

titans

TOOSH!

AAHHH!!

AAAHHH!!
OKAY, PREPARE FOR WARP SPEED.

WARP!
AAAHH!!

2½ DAYS LATER...

OPEN

AAAHH!!

DUDE, RELAX. WE'RE HERE.
OH, RIGHT. SORRY.

WATER. I NEED WATER.
C'MON, TITANS! LET'S GO MEET MY DAD!

NOW IT'S TIME TO CLEAN YOUR ROOM!

YOUR EARTH FRIENDS COULD HELP YOU!

PUT

CARRY

TOYS

PICK

DUST

SWEEP

SO, CLEANING YOUR **ROOM**, HUH?

I ALREADY **DID** MINE. SO... **NNYAH!**
WHO'S THAT?
OH, THAT'S MY SISTER. **HI BLACKFIRE.**
AREN'T YOUR FRIENDS A LITTLE **TOO FAR** AWAY FROM **HOME** FOR A LITTLE **TOO LONG?**

HUH? SHE'S RIGHT!
WE'VE BEEN GONE FOR TOO MANY DAYS!
WE'D BETTER GET HOME SOON OR WE'RE GONNA GET GROUNDED!

WHAT ARE WE GONNA DO?! WE HAVE TO GO BACK!

I'VE GOT AN IDEA!

DUST
PICK UP
CLEAN
FAST
SWEEP
CLEAN
FAST

THERE YA GO! JUST LIKE WE DO AT MY HOUSE!
TOYS
WHISPER
WHISPER
WHISPER

FWOOSH!
BONUS!
MINUTES LATER...
'BYE, DAD!
HAVE A GOOD TRIP, KIDS!
WE'LL KEEP DINNER WARM FOR YOU UNTIL YOU GET HOME!
YOU'RE COMING WITH, BLACKFIRE?
YEP!
I CAN'T WAIT TO SEE YOU TITANS GET GROUNDED!
YYAAHH!!!

2½ DAYS LATER...
YOU'RE GONNA GET IN TROUBLE!
YOU'RE GONNA GET IN TROUBLE!

TROUBLE... TROUBLE-TROUBLE!
AW, MAN!
SHE'S RIGHT!
WE'D BETTER THINK OF SOMETHING!

HI TITANS!
SUPERGIRL!
CAN YOU DO US A FAVOR?

WHISPER WHISPER WHISPER

OH! FLY AROUND THE EARTH BACKWARDS AND REVERSE TIME?
NO PROBLEM!

WOOSH!

SPIN
REVERSE
WHOOSH
AXIS
REVERSE
REVERSE
SPIN
WHOOSH
REVERSE

THERE YOU GO! ALL SET!
COOL!

YOU MEAN, YOU **TITANS** ARE **NOT** IN TROUBLE ANY MORE?

NOPE!

SUPERGIRL TURNED BACK **TIME** TO THE MOMENT **BEFORE** WE WENT INTO **SPACE!**

YYAAYYY!!

AW YEAH TITANS!
I WANT TO WELCOME EVERYONE TO THE FIRST OFFICIAL MEETING OF THE BIRD SCOUTS!
CAN WE HAVE A ROLLCALL PLEASE?
I'M HAWK!
DOVE!
RAVEN.
TALON!
tiny titans
TALON? AREN'T YOU FROM EARTH 53 OR SOMETHING?
I'M IN YOUR WORLD NOW, WONDER BREAD!
UM, IT'S BOY WONDER. AS IN ROBIN THE BOY WONDER!
YEAH? WHATEVER, DUDE.
ROBIN? I THOUGHT YOU WERE NIGHTWING!
NO, NOT ANYMORE.
WELL, WHO'S NIGHTWING? SOMEONE HAS TO BE NIGHTWING!
WAIT A MINUTE! IS NIGHTWING EVEN A BIRD?
RAVEN, WHAT DO YOU THINK?
KICK HIM OUT.

WHAT?!
BUT RAVEN! WE'RE ON THE SAME TEAM!
OUT.

HEY RAVEN, I LIKE YOUR STYLE...

AZARATH... METRION...

OKAY! OKAY!

THE FIRST OFFICIAL MEETING OF THE BIRD SCOUTS IS OFFICIALLY OVER.
HE **IS** A BIRD!
NO, HE'S **NOT**!
HE'S A WING!
A CHICKEN WING?
A KNIGHT'S WING?
CAN WE **GO** NOW?

tiny titans
"TO GET TO THE OTHER SIDE"

Hhmm...
SO, LET ME KNOW IF YOU HEARD THIS ONE...

THERE'S THIS CHICKEN, AND HE WANTED TO GET TO THE OTHER SIDE OF THE ROAD...
NO WAIT! ... YEAH, THAT'S RIGHT!
THEN HE CROSSED THE STREET... AND HE WAS WHERE HE WANTED TO BE IN THE FIRST PLACE!

YEAH, REAL FUNNY, MR. SMARTY PANTS!

OH YEAH...
REAL FUNNY, MR. SMARTY DRESS!

IT'S NOT A DRESS!
IT'S A ROBE!

YEAH, A PINK ROBE!
WAY TO GO, BRAINIAC!
OH, FORGET IT!

tiny titans

SPECIAL PIN-UP BY

FRANCO AURELIANI!

REPORT CARD PICKUP!

tiny titans

UM... WATCH OUT FOR MY TRICYCLE!

OH, THE INVISIBLE ONE, RIGHT?

tiny titans
HELLO, PARENTS AND STUDENTS...
...WELCOME TO REPORT CARD PICKUP!
PLEASE LINE UP FOR YOUR PARENT-TEACHER CONFERENCES...

BOTH ROBIN AND BARBARA EXCEL AT RIDDLES AND PUZZLE SOLVING!
PRINCIPAL SLADE
EXCELLENT IN GYMNASTICS, TOO.

KID FLASH NEEDS TO SLOW DOWN AND PAY MORE ATTENTION.
PRINCIPAL SLADE
HE SEEMS TO BREEZE THROUGH HIS HOMEWORK!

WONDER GIRL'S A WONDERFUL STUDENT!
PRINCIPAL SLADE
HER ANSWERS ARE VERY TRUTHFUL!

AQUALAD'S KNOWLEDGE OF THE WORLD'S OCEANS IS INCREDIBLE!
PRINCIPAL SLADE
HOWEVER, HE TAKES WAY TOO MANY WATER BREAKS THROUGHOUT THE DAY!

I DON'T MEAN TO SOUND **CLICHÉ**... SUPERGIRL'S GRADES ARE **SUPER**!
THAT'S **SUPER**!
REAL REAL **SUPER**!

HI, DAD!
HOW ARE OUR GRADES?
STRAIGHT A'S ... AS... USUAL!
GOOD JOB, ROSE!
GOOD JOB, JERICHO!

SPEEDY IS RIGHT ON TARGET.
PRINCIPAL SLADE

HELLO, MR. TRIGON. HERE'S RAVEN'S HONOR ROLL GRADES ONCE AGAIN!
LET'S HOPE SHE KEEPS THIS UP!
OH, SHE WILL... AT LEAST 'TIL THE END OF THE WORLD! HA HA HEE HOH!

I SUGGEST YOU HAVE A TALK WITH DUELA...
SHE'S DEFINITELY THE CLASS CLOWN.
PRINCIPAL SLADE

QUESTIONS, ENIGMA...
SO MANY QUESTIONS.
PRINCIPAL SLADE

BLUE BEETLE NEEDS HELP WITH ALL HIS SUBJECTS.
MAYBE A LITTLE HELP FROM HIS FRIENDS?
PRINCIPAL SLADE
IMAGINE THAT!
I KNOW, I KNOW. SOMETIMES THEY GO ON LIKE THIS ALL DAY.

MEANWHILE AT SIDEKICK CITY PRESCHOOL...
I KNOW MISS MARTIAN'S VERY GREEN, I MEAN, NEW, TO THE SCHOOL...
... BUT SHE'S ADAPTING VERY WELL.
MR. CLOCK KING

KID DEVIL DID REMARKABLY WELL ON HIS FIRE SAFETY EXAM!
MR. CLOCK KIN
CONGRATS!

LET'S HOPE OUR NEW STUDENTS WILL NOT BE LITTLE TERRORS!
WELCOME... LI'L DISRUPTOR
DREADBOLT
MISS PERSUADER
AND COPPERHEAD.
AW YEAH TERROR TITANS!

tiny titans
HI BEETLE.
HI STARFIRE!
"HAPPY FEELING BLUE"

CHEW
CHEW
CHEW

AW, WHY ARE YOU SO SAD?
SAD? I'M NOT SAD.
YES, YOU ARE.

WHY ARE YOU SO BLUE?
BLUE? BLUE IS THE COLOR OF MY COSTUME.
I HAVE TO BE BLUE SO I COULD BE CALLED BLUE BEETLE.

BUT BLUE IS SO SAD.
HOW ABOUT WE BRIGHTEN YOU UP WITH MORE CHEERY COLORS.

YOU DON'T WANT TO LOOK SAD ON YOUR BIRTHDAY!
BUT I'M NOT SAD.
BUT YOU LOOK IT!
WAIT, STAR! CAN WE TALK ABOUT THIS FIRST?

MINUTES LATER...
OOOHH! LOOK HOW HAPPY YOU ARE!
I FEEL LIKE COTTON CANDY.
GEE THANKS, BACKPACK!
PINK!

tiny titans
WAYNE
in...
"JOKE'S ON YOU"

OPEN
ROBIN
WAYNE MANOR
WAYN

OH ROBIN!
YOU HAVE MAIL!
ROBIN

IT SEEMS YOU AND MISS BARBARA HAVE BEEN INVITED TO A BIRTHDAY PARTY.

THANKS PENGUIN
BIRTHDAY? OOH... REALLY?

WHOSE PARTY?
WHOSE PARTY?
THE BLUE BEETLE.
OH BOY!
CAN'T WAIT!

I'M NOT GOING.
WHY NOT?
BLUE BEETLE'S BIRTHDAY! HAPPY THE CLOWN
CLOWNS!
IT SAYS THERE'S GOING TO BE A CLOWN THERE!
A CLOWN?
SO WHAT?

I HAVE BAD EXPERIENCES WITH CLOWNS!
HUH? WHAT ARE YOU TALKING ABOUT?
BLUE BEETLE'S BIRTHDAY! HAPPY THE CLOWN

UM, DOES THE NAME JOKER MEAN ANYTHING TO YOU?
JOKER IS A CLOWN! AND CLOWNS ARE BAD NEWS!
LEMME SEE THAT!
BLUE BEETLE'S BIRTHDAY! HAPPY THE CLOWN

BLUE BEETLE'S BIRTHDAY! HAPPY THE CLOWN

THIS GUY'S NAME IS HAPPY! HAPPY THE CLOWN.
YEAH WELL, YOU CAN'T BE TOO SURE.

HERE...
BLUE BEETLE'S BIRTHDAY! HAPPY THE CLOWN
WAG
WAG

...ACE WILL PROTECT YOU!
LET'S GO TO THE PARTY!

HERE'S SOME LEMONADE, CHILDREN.

THANK YOU, MR. BEETLE.

WOW! A GALLON OF BLUE PAINT! THANKS, BACKPACK!

AW YEAH TITANS!

WHO WANTS TO LAUGH?!

YAY! HAPPY THE CLOWN!

OH NO! THERE HE IS!
IT'S THE JOKER!
ROBIN, I'M NOT SURE IT'S...
IT'S HIM!

HE HAS THE SAME CRAZY PURPLE SUIT!
THE SAME BIG CREEPY ORANGE BOW TIE!

THE SAME SCARY GREEN HAIR!

LOOK OUT! HERE HE COMES!
HE'S ABOUT TO STRIKE!

GOTCHER NOSE!

YEAH, REAL DIABOLICAL!

SKIP

DANCE

HOP

QUICK! CALL THE COMMISSIONER!

GOTCHA!

tiny titans "BOOK SMARTS"
C'MON BUMBLEBEE, YOU COULD HELP ME RESEARCH FOR MY BUTTERFLY REPORT!

BUTTERFLIES!
BUTTERFLIES
HERE IT IS!
BUTTER-FLIES

RUMBLE
SHAKE
RUMBLE

POP!

POP
POP
POP!

BEAST BOY?
I MUST HAVE FALLEN ASLEEP DURING MY BUTTERFLY HOMEWORK.

WELL, THAT'S ONE WAY TO GET LOST IN A BOOK!
READIN'.

AW YEAH titans!
WELCOME TO OUR FIRST MEETING OF PET CLUB ATLANTIS!

PLEASE EXCUSE MY HOME. IT'S A LITTLE WET!
HEE HEE.

LET'S WELCOME OUR NEWEST MEMBER, LAGOON BOY!
AND HIS PETS...
JEREMY the JELLYFISH!
AND JIMMY the MUSSEL!

HI LAGOON BOY!

HI JEREMY!

AW YEAH THE MUSSEL!

GOOD TO SEE STREAKY AT A PET CLUB ATLANTIS MEETING!

YEP, HE NEEDS A FULL BODY WET SUIT...

...Y'KNOW HOW SUPERCATS HATE WATER!

IT'S THE ANT! HE WANTS TO JOIN!

ANT

REEL
REEL

WHAT'S THE NOTE SAY?
AFTER WHAT HAPPENED LAST TIME...
...YOU'RE NOT ALLOWED.

OH C'MON!
NO DUDE, YOU KNOW THE RULES.
ANT

I KNOW, I KNOW. FIRST RULE OF PET CLUB...
WE DON'T TALK ABOUT PET CLUB.
EXACTLY!
END!

tiny titans Puzzler!
WHAT PREHISTORIC ANIMAL DID BEAST BOY TURN INTO?
CONNECT THE DOTS TO FIND OUT!
POP
START
FINISH!
BONUS!
BLUE BEETLE'S BACKPACK LANGUAGE TRANSLATION!

BONUS PIN-UP!
ART BALTAZAR 2008!
tiny titans

SO, WHY ARE WE ALL MONKEYS?
EVENTUALLY, IT HAPPENS TO EVERYONE IN THIS UNIVERSE!
C'MON GUYS! IT'S NOT THAT BAD!
ART BALTAZAR 2008

tiny titans

WOW!

WHO'S THIS LITTLE GUY? HE'S SSOOOOO CUTE!

WHY DIDN'T YOU BRING HIM AROUND BEFORE?

EARTH ROCKS

THIS WILL BE THE LAST TIME, THAT'S FOR SURE!

SPEEDY

AW YEAH TITANS!

HI ROBIN!

I BROUGHT MARKERS!

I BROUGHT PAPER!

I WANNA MAKE MY OWN COMIC!

I BROUGHT BAGS AND BOARDS!

WE CAN'T WAIT TO SEE YOUR COLLECTION!

COOL. LET'S GO!

HAVE FUN, KIDS. I'LL BE RIGHT BACK WITH SOME GOODIES.

COMICS

CHECK THIS OUT! I CREATED MY OWN SUPERHERO!
HE LOOKS JUST LIKE BATMAN.
HEY! HERE'S A COMIC ABOUT SIDEKICKS!
REALLY? AM I IN THERE?
COMICS

HERE ARE SOME BANANA MUFFINS FOR YOU KIDS!
THANKS ALFRED!

Y'KNOW, SOMETIMES SIDEKICKS CAN BE COUSINS OF REAL SUPERHEROES!
YEP! AND SOMETIMES THEIR PETS ARE HEROES TOO!
EEP?

TWWWWZZAP!

HERE'S SOME ICY COLD MILK TO WASH DOWN THOSE GOODIES!

WELL, THAT EXPLAINS WHY THE BANANA MUFFINS WENT SO FAST.
WHAT THE--?

tiny titans
COLOR
OH. TIME TO WATER THE FLOWERS!
HEY! WATCH IT! WHO TURNED ON THE WATER?!
WELL, HONEY, THE WEATHERMAN DID SAY THERE MAY BE A CHANCE OF RAIN.

HUH? WHO SAID THAT?
WHO ARE YOU GUYS?
DOWN HERE!

HI. I'M THE ATOM!
MY WIFE MRS. ATOM...
OUR BABY SMIDGEN...
MY DAUGHTER DOT...
MY SON CRUMB...
...AND OUR DOG SPOT!

WHO ARE YOU TALKING TO, BEE?
THE ATOM AND HIS FAMILY.

THE ATOM'S FAMILY?
YOU GUYS ARE TINY!
REAL REAL TINY!
WE'RE TINY TINY TITANS!
AW YEAH TITANS!
SO ANYWAY, WE'RE TRYING TO HAVE A FAMILY PICNIC.
COULD YOU MAKE IT NOT RAIN ON US?

WAIT! I HAVE A SOLUTION!

COLOR

MINUTES LATER...

THANKS, BARBARA! THANKS, BUMBLEBEE!

SEE, MY LOVE. IT TURNED OUT TO BE A GREAT DAY AFTER ALL!

CAN YOU PASS ME ONE OF THOSE GRAPES?

RIGHT ON!

tiny titans
"MONKEY MAGIC" PART TWO
WALK
WALK
ROLL

TRAMPLE
TROT
JOG
MARCH
RUN
MONKEY

WHAT THE--?! WERE THOSE THE TITANS?
SURE LOOKED LIKE IT.
WERE THEY MONKEYS?
YEP.

UM... BRAIN?

NO! I DON'T WANT A BANANA!

WELL, MALLAH, IF YOU HANG OUT WITH THOSE GUYS...

...WHO AM I SUPPOSED TO HANG OUT WITH?

HI GUYS! HOW'S IT GOING?

TAP
WHEW! THAT WAS CLOSE.

HERE YOU GO.

titans
tiny titans
"MONKEY MAGIC"
PART 3

SO TELL US AGAIN WHY YOU GUYS ARE MONKEYS.

OH, HI BEPPO!
HOW ARE YOU?
WOULD YOU LIKE SOME CEREAL?

TWIZZZAAAH!

WELL, TECHNICALLY, WE'RE CHIMPANZEES.
I'M HUNGRY.
WHO WANTS BANANAS?

tiny titans
WELCOME TO OUR FIRST OFFICIAL MEETING OF THE TITANS APES!

I'M SURE YOU ALL KNOW MALLAH, CO-FOUNDER OF TITANS APES!
YAH YAH YAH YAH YAH YAH

YES, BEPPO? DID YOU HAVE SOMETHING TO ADD TO OUR MEETING?

WOW, BEPPO! YOU DID IT!
I'M MYSELF AGAIN!

TWWZZZAH!

tiny titans
RAVEN?
HEY.

WHAT ARE YOU DOING HERE?

I'M BABYSITTING KID DEVIL.
FIRST, I TOOK HIM TO MY HOUSE...

...BUT HE MADE MY DAD ACT CRAZY!
HE'S GREAT! I LOVE THIS LITTLE GUY!
HE'S NOT A BABY, DAD! I'M JUST WALKING HIM HOME FROM SCHOOL!

SO ANYWAY, I HEARD YOU GUYS WERE MONKEYS.
YEAH! BEPPO GOT HOLD OF ZATARA'S WAND AND...

I'LL TAKE CARE OF IT... AZARATH...
METRION... ZINTHOS!

WOW!
THANKS, RAVEN!
NO PROBLEM. LATER, TITANS.

THAT WAS REAL COOL OF RAVEN TO HELP US OUT!
ZAP
AW YEAH! LET'S SEE WHAT'S ON TV.
CLICK
OH, I LOVE THIS EPISODE!

TWIZZAP! TWIZZAP!

WAIT A MINUTE. WHAT JUST HAPPENED?
SEE THE GUY WITH THE BLACK HAT? HE'S THE BAD GUY.
OH, THIS MAKES MUCH MORE SENSE NOW!
-END!

tiny titans Puzzler!

WELCOME TO THE
PET CLUB
WORD SEARCH!

E	F	E	S	O	C	S	P	K	G	L	Q	H	Q	U
L	R	C	Y	P	R	R	N	N	A	C	A	P	L	A
I	F	A	Z	P	L	J	F	E	H	O	C	R	J	C
Z	D	L	Z	E	L	O	I	A	V	N	C	F	R	O
A	Q	X	I	B	W	E	K	B	K	A	N	L	X	C
B	R	R	D	S	N	B	M	A	Q	M	R	E	Q	O
E	Q	K	C	L	E	S	S	U	M	Y	M	M	I	J
T	S	T	R	E	A	K	Y	U	K	B	E	T	M	A
H	S	A	N	P	E	T	C	L	U	B	W	K	R	O
X	K	Y	R	T	A	S	O	Q	Y	Q	Y	O	R	X
C	X	O	W	U	E	M	J	M	T	F	B	Q	R	F
K	R	J	X	V	D	P	F	R	W	I	F	M	Q	L
P	L	R	N	S	N	I	U	G	N	E	P	U	J	D
H	A	Y	X	L	I	K	Y	S	V	U	C	V	L	P
E	Q	C	U	V	G	R	J	L	X	D	D	X	F	F

Find these words in the puzzle above!

~~PETCLUB~~
ELIZABETH
BEPPO
RAVENS
PENGUINS
STREAKY
FLUFFY
ACE
ROBINS
COCO
JIMMYMUSSEL
ALPACA

AW YEAH TITANS!

BONUS PIN-UP!
tiny tiny titans
the ATOM
DOT
MRS. ATOM
SMIDGEN
CRUMB
SPOT
THE ATOM'S FAMILY
ART BALTAZAR 2008!

ART BALTAZAR
2008!
WORLD'S FUNNEST!

tiny titans

SO, LET ME GET THIS STRAIGHT... THESE BIRDS CAN'T FLY? BUT THE HORSE, CAT, AND MONKEY CAN?

YES, THAT'S CORRECT.

ROBIN

STARFIRE

RAVEN

KID FLASH

MISS MARTIAN

KID DEVIL

CASSIE

BEAST BOY

AQUALAD

WONDER GIRL

BUMBLEBEE

CYBORG

ROSE

SPEEDY

MEANWHILE IN THE ARCTIC...
tiny titans IN "TEA TIME"
COUSIN KAL?

YES?
SUPER DOG FOOD
KRYPTO

CAN I GO PLAY WITH THE TITANS TODAY?

HMM...
OKAY. DON'T COME HOME TOO LATE. ALSO, REMEMBER TO FEED YOUR CAT, STREAKY.
GREAT!
KRYPTO

KRYPTO
STREAKY
KRYPTO
STREAKY
STREAKY
GROWL
!

MEANWHILE IN GOTHAM CITY...

DAD!
MAY I GO TO TITANS TREEHOUSE TODAY?
YES, DEAR. HAVE FUN.

COOL!
THANKS POP!

DON'T FORGET TO FEED ACE BEFORE YOU LEAVE!

PRESS

BBZZZZZ
OPEN

RIDE
ACE

ACE

ACE
GROWL
ACE
LEAP!

titans
MEANWHILE AT TITANS TREEHOUSE...

AW YEAH TITANS!

HUH?
WHERE DID EVERYBODY GO?

AW YEAH TITANS!

HI BARBARA.
HI SUPERGIRL! WHERE ARE THE TITANS?
I DON'T KNOW. THEY'RE NOT HERE.
HMM.
WHAT DO YOU WANT TO DO NOW?
YOU WANT TO HAVE A TEA PARTY?
OOH YEAH! THAT SOUNDS LIKE FUN!
UM... WHERE?
I KNOW! WE COULD GO TO GOTHAM CITY!
OKAY! LET'S GO!
titans

titans

titans

MMEOW?

ARF
ARF
ARF

MMRRRROOWW
GRrrrr...

GROWL
GROWL

STREAKY
ACE

MEANWHILE BACK IN GOTHAM CITY...
WOULD YOU LIKE MORE TEA, MR. TEDDY?
HOW ABOUT YOU, MR. BUNNY?

RATTTLE
RATTLE
CRASH
BANG
RATTLE
CAN

RATTLE
RATTLE
GARBAGE
KROC

BAM
BAM
BAM!

SHAKE
SHAKE

GRAB

TOSS
EAT

CHOMP
CHEW

SLAM!

KROC
EEEOOOWW!
THAT'S GROSS!
YUCK!
DISGUSTING!
NASTY!

LET'S HAVE OUR TEA PARTY SOME PLACE ELSE!
YEAH, SOMEPLACE WHERE PEOPLE DON'T EAT GARBAGE!
HOW ABOUT METROPOLIS?
OKAY, LET'S GO!

ZIP!

KROC

TOSS
ZIP
FLY

CHEW
CHEW
MMM

MEANWHILE IN METROPOLIS...
HERE'S A GOOD SPOT FOR OUR TEA PARTY!

LET'S HOPE THERE'S NOT A GARBAGE-EATING KROC MONSTER HERE!

HAVE SOME TEA, MR. BUNNY.
COOKIE, MR. TEDDY?

CRUNCH
CRUNCH

CHIPS
HEY! WATCH IT! YOU'RE GETTING YOUR CRUMBS ALL OVER US!

HUH? GOODBYE TITANS! BIZARRO AM NOT SORRY! VERY UNTASTY! BIZARRO NOT LIKE BAD CHIPS! NOT FAVORITE!
CHIPS

CHIPS

THIS GUY, BIZARRO, MAKES NO SENSE!
HE SPEAKS OPPOSITE OR SOMETHING!

CRUNCH CRUNCH

LET'S GO SOMEPLACE WHERE NO ONE CRUNCHES CHIPS ON US!
CHIPS

FLY
ZIP

CHEW
CRUNCH

?

YAH! THE GIRLS DID NOT FLY THAT WAY!

ZIP

!

MEANWHILE IN A NICE QUIET PARK...
MMM... THIS TEA IS LOVELY.
SIP
FINALLY, SOME PEACE AND QUIET!
HOW'S YOUR TEA, MR. BUNNY?
WWWAAAAAHH
SNIFF WHIMPER SNIFF
AGAIN?
WHAT THE--?
THAT SOUNDS LIKE CRYING!
WE CAN'T HAVE A TEA PARTY WITH SOMEONE CRYING!
C'MON! WE'RE SUPERHEROES!
WE HAVE TO FIND OUT WHO IS SO SAD!
ACE?
STREAKY?
WHIMPER WHIMPER
WHIMPER SOB SOB

GROWL
GROWL
GROWL

OH MY GOSH!
DID WE FORGET TO FEED YOU?

WELL, I THINK THERE ARE TWO MORE GUESTS WE SHOULD INVITE TO OUR TEA PARTY!

MINUTES LATER...
WOULD YOU LIKE SOME MORE TEA, MR. TEDDY?
HOW ABOUT YOU, MR. BUNNY?
CHEW EAT MUNCH
ACE
STREAKY

HOW ABOUT YOU, MR. KROC?
ANOTHER COOKIE, MR. BIZARRO?
YUM.
ACE
STREAKY
—AW YEAH TITANS!
THE END!

tiny titans
WORD LINK PUZZLER
TITANSLADELIZABETHOTSPOTRIGONIGHTWINGIZMOCTOPUSHIMMEROSENIGMANTERRAQUALADUELALFREDOVELEMENTARYELLOWILDEBEESTEACHAWKRYPTORANGELEPHANTITANS!

BONUS
PIN-UP!
titans
FRANCO8

OH, TERRA! LET ME COUNT THE WAYS!
YOU CAN START BY COUNTING THESE ROCKS!
ART BALTAZAR 2008!
TERRA
GIRL TROUBLE!

tiny titans

SEE, I TOLD YOU NIGHTWING WAS A BIRD!

ROBIN

STARFIRE

RAVEN

INERTIA

MISS MARTIAN

KID DEVIL

CASSIE

BEAST BOY

SUPERGIRL

WONDER GIRL

BARBARA

CYBORG

BLUE BEETLE

SPEEDY

tiny titans
IN
"COUNTING ON LOVE ROCKS!"

HI TERRA!

I WROTE A POEM FOR YOU!

ROSES ARE RED, VIOLETS ARE BLUE. SUGAR IS SWEET...
...AND YOUR HAIR IS AS COOL AS RAINBOW SHERBERT WITH A DOLLOP OF WHIPCREAM AND A SPOON!

WHAT?
WHAT KIND OF POEM IS THAT?! IT DIDN'T EVEN RHYME! WHY WOULD I PUT A SPOON IN MY HAIR, YOU FREAK?!

OH, TERRA... HOW DO I LOVE THEE? LET ME COUNT THE WAYS!

ONE!

ROCK!

TWO.

ROCK!
STONE!

THREE?

ROCK
QUARRY!
FLINT!

DUDE, I THINK YOU'D BETTER STOP COUNTING.
MY LOVE KNOWS NO BOUNDARIES...

tiny titans
IN
"NAME EXCHANGE"
HI.
HELLO.
MY NAME IS ROBIN! YOU'RE NEW AROUND HERE, AREN'T YOU?
YEP. I'M THE NEW FOREIGN EXCHANGE STUDENT!
MY NAME IS STARFIRE!
PLEASE TO MEET YOU...
...STARFIRE?
WAIT A MINUTE... WE ALREADY HAVE A STARFIRE!
SO?

HMM... THAT'S GOING TO CAUSE PROBLEMS FOR YOU.
YOU'RE PROBABLY GOING TO HAVE TO CHANGE YOUR NAME.
WHY?

HI, ROBIN!

HI, NIGHTWING!

HI, NIGHTLIGHT!

HI, ICE BUCKET!

SEE, STUFF LIKE THAT HAPPENS.
ALL I DID WAS CHANGE MY COSTUME ONCE AND...
...HERE!
LET'S TRY SOMETHING AND WATCH WHAT HAPPENS!
AW YEAH TITANS! THIS IS MY NEW FRIEND STARFIRE!!

HOW ARE YOU, STARFIRE?

WHAT'S UP, STARFIRE?

WOW! THAT'S SO COOL! MY NAME IS STARFIRE TOO!
IT IS?

HMM... HOW ABOUT I CHANGE MY NAME TO REDSTAR THEN?

OOH REDSTAR! I LIKE THE NAME REDSTAR!
IT SOUNDS COOL!
THANKS, TITANS!

SLADE'S OFFI
BYE, REDSTAR!

SEE YA, REDSTAR!

SLADE'S OFFICE
NICE TO MEET YOU, REDSTAR!

SEE YOU AT LUNCH, REDSTAR!

ELEME

WELL, THANKS FOR INTRODUCING ME TO ALL MY NEW FRIENDS!
AND, THANK YOU FOR ALL THE GOOD ADVICE!

OH, YOU'RE WELCOME! IT WAS NICE TO MEET YOU, REDSTAR!
NICE TO MEET YOU, TOO.

SLADE'S OFFICE
SEE YOU LATER, ICE BUCKET!
-CHILLIN'

tiny titans
IN "ROCK DOG"
COOL. HERE COMES TERRA!

POP!
POP!

OH, LOOK AT THE CUTE LITTLE PUPPY!

WAIT A MINUTE... WHY IS HE GREEN?

UHNG! MAYBE SHE'S A CAT PERSON.
-OUCH.

tiny titans
SORRY, KID. YOU GOTTA BE AT LEAST THIS TALL TO RIDE THIS RIDE.
MERRY GO 'ROUND RIDES

RUN RUN
MERRY GO 'ROUN RID
SKIP
SCAMP

ENJOY.
MERRY GO 'ROUND RIDES
-HELMET!

OH NO, HERE COMES THAT BEAST BOY KID AGAIN.
tiny titans
IN
"ROCK SHOW"
TERRA! TERRA!

HI TERRA!

WHAT?!
I'M JUST THROWING OUT IDEAS HERE!
-SIGH!

tiny titans
IN "DOUBLE FEATURE"
BLOB MONSTER
GREAT WHITE SHARK
TICKETS

HELP! HELP! MONSTER!
AAHH! YYAHH!
MONSTER
WHITE SHARK
TICKETS

BLOB MONSTER
GREAT WHITE SHARK
TICKETS

YOU CAN'T BLAME THEM. YOU DO LOOK ALOT LIKE THAT BLOB MONSTER.
PLASMUS THINKS WEARING THAT SHARK FIN DIDN'T HELP US NEITHER.
—POPCORN.

tiny titans
IN
"ROCKET BOX"

HI, BEAST BOY. WHAT ARE YOU DOING?
I'M GOING TO TEST OUT MY ROCKET BOX!

DRESSED LIKE SUPERMAN?
I TOLD YOU, TERRA'S NOT INTO GREEN DUDES!
YOU'RE WASTING YOUR TIME.
NONSENSE.

HI BEAST BOY! WHATCHA GOT THERE?
MY SUPER SPACESHIP ROCKETBOX!

HI TERRA! WANNA GO FOR A RIDE IN MY SPACE SHIP?
YOU'RE TOO CLOSE.

CLICK CLICK CLICK

UM... IT'S NOT GOING ANYWHERE, BEAST BOY.
IT'S JUST A BOX.
MAYBE WE SHOULD HELP HIM PUSH.
CLICK CLICK CLICK

WHAT THE?!
CYBORG SAID THIS WOULD WORK!

STOP WASTING MY TIME, BEAST BOY!
LATER, LOSERS.

CLICK
CLICK

HHMM... LEMME TAKE A LOOKSEE.

HERE'S THE PROBLEM. THE SAFETY'S ON!
CLICK
OFF

FOOSH!!

WELL ANYWAY, WHO WANTS TACOS?
YEAH, I COULD USE ONE.

WILL BEAST BOY MEET US THERE?
MAYBE WE SHOULD GET HIM SOMETHING "TO GO".
-LET'S EAT!

tiny titans Presents... "the Kroc files"
IN "CHANGING A LIGHTBULB"

tiny titans Puzzler!
CAN YOU HELP BEAST BOY FIND HIS WAY TO TERRA?
-AW YEAH TITANS!

SUPER BONUS PIN-UP!
to my Good
ART BALTAZAR 2008
ALFRED and the PENGUINS

YOUR FACE.
NO, YOUR FACE!
WORLD'S BEST PRINCIPAL
ART BALTAZAR 2008
FACES OF MISCHIEF!

tiny titans

MASTER ROBIN, THERE'S A GENTLEMAN HERE WHO CLAIMS THE PENGUINS BELONG TO HIM.

WHAT PENGUINS?

BEAST BOY

SUPERGIRL

MISS MARTIAN

KID DEVIL

CYBORG

BLUE BEETLE

SPEEDY

tiny titans
IN
"MORNING WITH
THE TRIGONS"

SEE YA IN
SCHOOL,
CUPCAKE!

DAD!

YES,
SWEETIE-
PIE?

ARE YOU SUBBING TODAY?

WELL, YES I AM.
YOU'RE WEARING THE WRONG OUTFIT AGAIN.

HUH? WHA?

OH RIGHT! THIS IS MY "TAKING OVER THE WORLD" OUTFIT! SILLY ME!
GOOD CALL, BUTTERCUP!
THIS WAS ALMOST EMBARRASSING!

SEE YA IN SCHOOL.
YEP.
-SUIT!

tiny titans
IN
"MONDAY MORNING"
PRINCIPAL SLADE'S OFFICE
YELL YELL! BLAH BLAH!
SCOLD! SHOUT SCOLD! BLAH BLAH!

YES, SIR. YOU'RE ABSOLUTELY RIGHT.
GUINEA PIGS AND HAMSTERS ARE NOT THE SAME.

OH, MR. TRIGON? ARE YOU NEXT?
GOOD LUCK.

PRINCIPAL SLADE'S OFFICE

WELL, ARE YOU COMING IN, OR ARE YOU GOING TO SIT OUT THERE ALL DAY?

WELL, UM, Y'SEE, UM...
OUT WITH IT, TRIGON!
PRINCIPAL SLADE

Y'SEE, I HAVE THESE BASEBALL TICKETS...
MR. TRIGON...
DO YOU WANT TO TAKE ME TO A BASEBALL GAME?
YES, SIR.

PRINCIPAL SLADE

OKAY, HOLD ON A SECOND.
BBZZ BZZZ

MEANWHILE IN THE SCHOOL CAFETERIA...
BBZZZ BBZZZ

YEAH?

MR. DARKSEID, MAY I SEE YOU IN MY OFFICE, PLEASE?

YEAH.

SPLAT!

MINUTES LATER...

YOU WANTED TO SEE ME, SIR?

YES! MR. TRIGON HAS BROUGHT SOMETHING TO MY ATTENTION!

PRINCIPAL SLADE'S OFFICE
SNEAK
TIP TOE

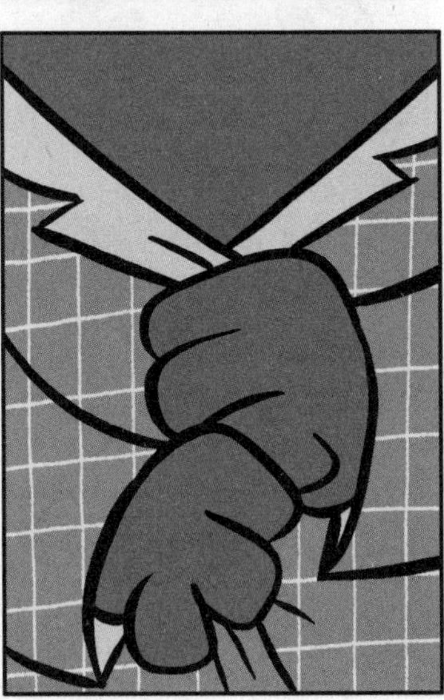

OH, IT'S ON!

SIDEKICK CITY ELEMENTARY

SIDEKICK CITY ELEMENTARY

SIDEKICK CITY ELEMENTARY

OOHH! DID YOU FEEL THAT?
SUDDENLY, THERE'S A COLD EVIL CHILL!
BRRR! I FELT IT TOO!
A DARK, BITTER, EVIL SHUDDER!

—CHILLAXIN'

tiny titans
IN "TAKE ME OUT TO THE BALLGAME"
MISS ROSE,
MISS RAVEN,
MR. SLADE AND MR. TRIGON ARE HERE FOR YOU.
MENTA
WHERE ARE WE GOING, DAD?
YOU'LL SEE.
DAD, WHERE'S YOUR JACKET?
DON'T NEED IT, HONEY.
SO, GIRLS, DO YOU LIKE BASEBALL?
C'MON, LET'S GO PICK UP YOUR BROTHER, JERICHO, FROM PRE-SCHOOL!
#1
the HIVE
YEAH, I KNOW. THE BIG RED GUY IS MY DAD.
4
BATTER UP!

tiny titans
ATTENTION STUDENTS! I, DARKSEID, YOUR ACTING PRINCIPAL OF THE DAY...
...HAS DECLARED THAT TODAY WE WILL TAKE OUR FINALS!
WHAT? BUT IT'S NOT EVEN THE END OF THE SEMESTER!
WE DIDN'T EVEN STUDY!
THIS IS SUCH A CRISIS!
THAT'S RIGHT! A FINALS CRISIS!
NO MORE MR. NICE GUY! TODAY, DARKSEID, HAS WON!
MAN, I LIKED DARKSEID BETTER WHEN HE WAS THE LUNCH LADY.
YEAH.

-INFINITE!

tiny titans

AW MAN, I SURE MISS MR. SLADE AS PRINCIPAL!

WHAT DO YOU SUPPOSE HE'S DOING RIGHT NOW?

FINAL

FINAL

YEAH, HE'S **PROBABLY** CREATING **MORE** HOMEWORK ASSIGNMENTS **AS WE SPEAK!**

YA-HOO!

AAAHHH!

AAHHH!!

HE'S PROBABLY GOING TO ELIMINATE RECESS!
YEAH.
ATTENTION STUDENTS!
THERE WILL BE MANDATORY DETENTION TODAY FOR THE ENTIRE SCHOOL!
DARKSEID HAS SPOKEN!
AW MAN!
THAT'S NOT FAIR!
I SURE MISS PRINCIPAL SLADE. HE WAS SO COOL.
-COW-A-BUNGA-

tiny titans
IN
"HALL PASS"
WALK
WALK

ELEMENTARY
EXCUSE ME? WHERE IS YOUR HALL PASS?
YEP! I AM THE MONITOR!
AND, WHILE I'M ON THE JOB, YOU'LL NEED A HALL PASS!
HALL PASS?

OH, I COULDN'T HELP OVERHEARING. LET THE BOY GO. HE DOESN'T NEED A HALL PASS.

SEZ WHO?
SAYS ME, THE ANTI-MONITOR.

-RUN, ROBIN, RUN!

tiny titans
IN "OUR LITTLE SECRET"
WOW! I CAN'T BELIEVE HOW COOL OUR DADS ARE!
TODAY WAS SSSOOOOO MUCH FUN!
I'M GOING TO TELL EVERYONE HOW FUN OUR DADS ARE!

EVERYONE?

JERICHO, CAN YOU...?

ZAP!
THIS IS OUR LITTLE SECRET.
OTHERS CAN NEVER KNOW ABOUT OUR DADS' COOLNESS.
WE WILL NEVER SPEAK OF THIS DAY AGAIN.
TODAY... DIDN'T... HAPPEN...
TODAY... DIDN'T... HAPPEN...
THAT'S BETTER.
-THINKING!

MR. DARKSEID...
YES?
DARKSEID
F
FAIL

MY JACKET PLEASE.
DARKS

GOOD JOB, DARKSEID... PLEASURE TO KNOW I CAN CALL UPON YOU WHEN NEEDED.
YOU KNOW WHERE TO FIND ME.

YES, MR. TRIGON?

SAME TIME NEXT WEEK?
YOU BETCHA.

AW YEAH TITANS!
#1
PRINCIPAL SLADE
-COOLNESS!

AND NOW... tiny titans Presents... "the Kroc files"

IN "SENDING AN E-MAIL"

the RIGHT WAY

TYPE KEY TYPE

TYPE TYPE KEY KEY PRESS TYPE PRESS

i Dan,
How are you?
Everything is
cool in the
Batcave.
Later,
Alfred

CLICK SEND!

mail
sent to
Dan.

the Kroc WAY

Daily Planet

tiny titans Puzzler!
BASEBALL UNSCRAMBLE
BOCOARRSED
OHEM 0 0 2 0 1
ISVTIRO 1 0 0 3
ATB
ATH
REHCCAT
the HIVE
the HIVE
TRTBAE
TMIT
MEHO LAPET
LBAL
AW YEAH TITANS!

SIDEKICK CITY ELEMENTARY
FACULTY
Mr. Trigon
Dr. Light
Mr. Darkseid
Principal Slade
ART BALTAZAR 2008!